Get **more** out of libraries

Please return or renew this item by the last date shown.

You can renew online at www.hants.gov.uk/library

Or by phoning 0300 555 1387

Hampshire
County Council

MIRKUCOURT

The Pirate's Daughter

By Christophe Miraucourt

Illustrated by Delphine Vaufrey

W

FRANKLIN WATTS

LONDON•SYDNEY

Meet the Crew

Ricky

Melinda

Gingerbeard

Fatbeak

CHAPTER 1
A Present for Gingerbeard

"Prepare to board, me hearties! Grab the

grappling hooks! Show no mercy!"

shouted Melinda the Terrible, waving

her wooden sword about on her father,

Gingerbeard's, ship.

"What are you doing?" her brother Ricky

asked with a snigger.

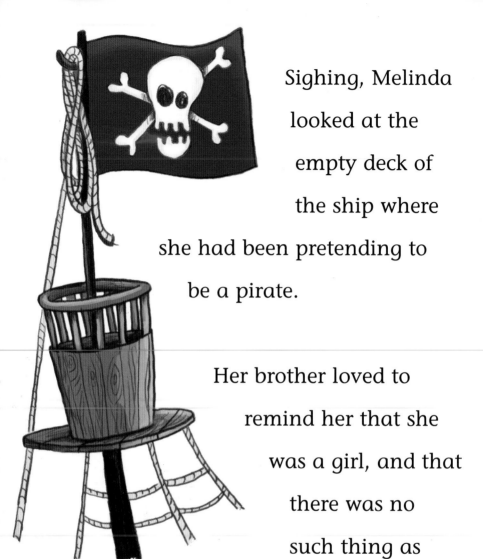

Sighing, Melinda looked at the empty deck of the ship where she had been pretending to be a pirate.

Her brother loved to remind her that she was a girl, and that there was no such thing as a girl pirate.

Even the daughter of one of the
greatest pirates in the history of
the seas was no exception!

Melinda still dreamed
about chasing
ships, exploring
treasure islands
and finding
treasure chests
full of gold!

But every time she asked Gingerbeard to take her with him, he just made excuses:

"You'd feel sea-sick!"

Or:

"You'd be so scared of the cannons firing that you wouldn't set foot on the deck!"

"Don't forget about Dad's birthday present," Ricky reminded her.

Oh dear. Melinda's heart sank.

 It was the same problem every year. What could you possibly get your pirate dad, who already had plenty of jewels and weapons?

"You could always make him another sculpture like last year!" Ricky teased her. Gingerbeard had barely looked at the pistol that she had carved in wood.

Ricky's present, the head of a shark with very long teeth, hung proudly on a wall in Gingerbeard's cabin.

"This year, I'll write Daddy a poem," Melinda decided. She would tell him how much she admired and loved him. "That's a rubbish present for a pirate!" said Ricky. Melinda shrugged her shoulders. She knew Gingerbeard would love it.

While her dad was getting ready for his next trip, Melinda ran off to the Port of Skull Island, where she hoped to find an old piece of parchment on which to write her poem. After much walking about and not much luck, Melinda was about to give up.

Then she stumbled upon a tiny shop

hidden between a hat shop and

a sword shop. Her eyes lit up – the

window was full of parchments!

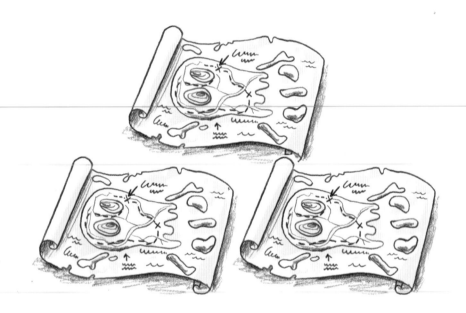

CHAPTER 2
The Map of Skull Island

As Melinda opened the door, a parrot

called Fatbeak squawked, "Land ahoy!" and

a scary-looking pirate came forward. He had

an eye patch and a squeaky wooden leg.

"What are you looking for?" he said,

studying Melinda from head to toe with

his only eye.

"A pa-pa...
parchment!"
Melinda stuttered.
"I'd like to write a
poem on it for my
daddy's birthday."

"Birthday!"repeated Fatbeak.
"I have just what you need!" said the pirate.
He searched inside an old dusty chest before
holding a parchment as wrinkled as his old
skin. Melinda was delighted. This was just
what she needed! She handed two coins to
the pirate and quickly went back home.

Melinda's house was in Shinbone's Cove, overlooking Shipwrecked Sea. It was a big log cabin, built in the shape of a ship, with a pirate flag swaying on the roof. Melinda sat down at the table, took out her goose-feather quill and dipped the nib in her bottle of squid ink. With her most perfect handwriting, she started writing:

Dear Daddy,

I will always love you,

I love your swords, and your

ginger beard too!

I am so proud to be your daughter,

You're the most perfect pirate father!

But before she could finish it, Ricky

snatched the parchment from her.

'Dear Daddeeeeey..." he read with a mocking laugh, "Oh I love you, I love you!" Melinda chased her brother, but Ricky forced her to stop when he held the parchment over a candle.

"If you move a single toe, I'll burn it," he threatened her.

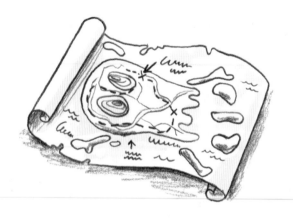

Melinda stood still: the light of the flame revealed the map of an island – their very own island!

Melinda grabbed the parchment back and ran to her bedroom, locking herself away.

A map in invisible ink meant precious treasure, Melinda thought. Her heart was racing. She studied the map. Somewhere in the north of Skull island, a chest had been drawn with an inscription underneath it:

Captain Sproggobbler's Treasure

Melinda shivered. Sproggobbler was the most terrifying pirate. He had disappeared ten years ago, following a galleon attack. Parents still told stories about him coming back to kidnap children who were naughty and didn't do as they were told.

"If you don't eat your seaweed soup," Gingerbeard sometimes threatened, "Captain Sproggobbler will get you!"

No one had ever found his treasure. Suddenly, the clue was here at Melinda's fingertips! She recognised one of the places on the map: Ghosts' Cliff. She knew how to get there. New treasure would make a lovely present for Dad, she decided.

"Dinner's ready!" Gingerbeard's voice boomed. Melinda hid the map under her pillow and joined her family at the kitchen table.

She was given a bowl of steaming crab soup and a plate of shark meat stew, her two favourite dishes!

Ricky tried to work out what Melinda was thinking. She poked out her tongue and he kicked her leg under the table. Then she pelted him with little balls of white bread.

That night, she fell asleep peacefully. When she woke up and slid her hand underneath her pillow, she realised with horror that the map had disappeared!

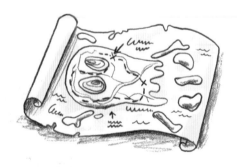

CHAPTER 3
Island of Danger

Melinda got up in a hurry. She knew Ricky had to be the thief! She rushed to his bedroom and found it empty. He must have got up very early to go after the treasure. Melinda didn't need the parchment: she had memorised the map and all its details.

She tied a scarf around her head.

Then she grabbed the sword that used to

belong to her grandfather, Blackbeard,

and stepped out of the house. The sun

hadn't risen yet and the only person in

sight was an old pirate taking his dog

for a walk.

A moon as round as a cannon ball lit Melinda's way to Ghosts' Cliff. There, she saw the two giant rocks she'd seen on the map blocking the way to the cave.

She had nearly missed them but a strip of Ricky's shirt had caught her eye. It meant that Ricky was ahead of her!

Melinda squeezed into the cave.
It was very dark inside and the
ground was covered with slippery
slime. She stepped onto a flat stone,
which she felt sinking under her.

At once, two howling
skeletons sprung
up in front of her!

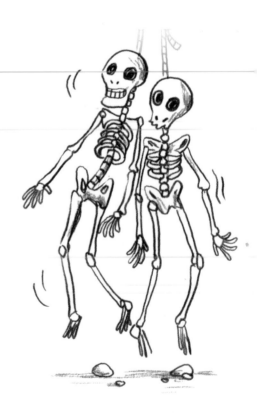

But Melinda didn't run away. Instead, she lifted her sword in front of her and shouted: "I am Melinda the Terrible, daughter of Gingerbeard, granddaughter of Blackbeard and great-granddaughter of Redbeard. I am not scared of you!"

Then, she closed her eyes and swung her sword around blindly. When she opened her eyes again, she found a pile of skeleton bones at her feet.

Melinda noticed that there were ropes connecting the skeletons to the ceiling of the cave. Stepping on the stone must have triggered the skeletons to drop down.

It must be Sproggobbler's little trick to scare people away! She secretly hoped that her brother's hair went white with fear.

Melinda hurried on, feeling her way out towards the daylight. She found herself on the other side of the cliff, on a side of the island she didn't know.

She remembered the directions on the map and turned right after the three palm trees which grew like intertwined swords. A small boat should have been hidden there.

If her memory was right, she would

need it to cross the Crocodile Marshes.

But there was no sign of the small boat.

Melinda realised that someone had cut

the rope which tied the boat to the trees.

She bent down and saw Ricky's pocket

knife! "Ricky may have my map, but

I won't let him steal my treasure!"

she declared.

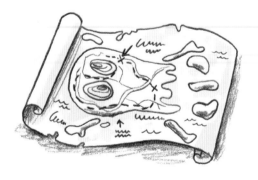

Melinda saw a few stepping stones across the marshes. She took a deep breath. As she jumped onto the first stone, she noticed that it was moving. She realised it was a crocodile!

The marshes were full of real crocodiles!

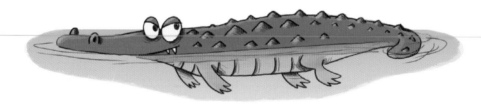

CHAPTER 4
The Chest at Serpent's Rock

Gingerbeard's daughter was not ready to give up. She jumped skilfully from one crocodile to the next and dodged every snapping jaw.

At last, she set foot on the other side of the marsh. As she began walking into the jungle, she heard a cry in the distance: "Help! Help!" It was Ricky's voice.

Melinda ran to the rescue. She found him at the bottom of a pit that had been hidden with twigs.

"You would have avoided this if you had known what the skull on the map meant," she told him.

"Just help me!" Ricky begged. "I'll give you the map back, I promise!"

Melinda paused. "Do you still feel the same way about girl pirates?" she asked.

Ricky thought for a while before replying. "I have to say that you are as brave and cunning as a pirate."

"I totally agree with you," Melinda responded proudly.

With Blackbeard's sword,
Melinda cut off a vine,
grabbed one end and threw
the other end down to Ricky.

Once free, Ricky
slowly handed
Melinda her map.
"Now, I won't have
a present for Daddy,"
he wailed.

Melinda looked at her brother and saw
how upset he was.

"Why don't we give Daddy the treasure
together?" she suggested.
"Are you sure?" said Ricky.
"Well, if we want to find it,
two pirates are better than one,"
she said. They studied the map.
A chest was drawn underneath
Serpent's Rock.

"Let's go!" Melinda cried. With her sword, she cut through the jungle.

Before long, they reached a clearing where a serpent-shaped rock stood. Ricky and Melinda shuddered.

Melinda quickly discovered that the rock had a huge gap underneath and she could see the chest.

"This is too easy. It must be a trap!" Thinking about their dad's birthday present made her feel braver.

She approached the chest when suddenly she heard a hissing sound. Melinda screamed with fear. Coming out of the rock were snakes, lots of snakes! Soon they were completely surrounded!

CHAPTER 5
Sproggobbler's Secret

"What do we do now?" Ricky mumbled.

"Any idea how to get us out of this?"

Melinda felt bad admitting that for the first

time, she didn't know what to do.

Suddenly, springing out of the jungle,

Gingerbeard appeared.

"Death to the snakes!" he howled.

With his sword, he defeated

each and every one of them.

"Daddy!" Ricky and Melinda cried together.

"How did you find us?"

"The old pirate with the dog you came across told me which way you went. He's an old friend."

Taking turns, Melinda and Ricky

told him about their trouble

with the skeletons, and

the crocodiles,

the trap in the jungle

and the snakes.

"I am so proud of you both," he said.

"You will become the greatest pirates of all

the seas. As for you," he added, squeezing

Melinda in his arms, "you showed that you

were worthy of Blackbeard's sword. It should

belong to you."

"Open the chest, Dad!" Melinda said,

full of pride. "It's your birthday present!"

Gingerbeard pulled the chest towards him

and with a swish of his sword, broke open

its lock. Ricky and Melinda held

their breath...

"Oooh!" Melinda cried in surprise.

"Uh?!" said Ricky. They couldn't believe
their eyes. Inside the chest lay an old
teddy bear with an eye patch. Not a
single gold bar or silver coin, or even
the tiniest jewel.

"What is this all about?" Ricky said,

disappointed.

"Where's the treasure?" Melinda

complained.

"Kids, this is Sproggobbler's treasure!"

Gingerbeard said. "For him, this teddy was

the most precious of all things because it

reminded him of his childhood."

"But now we don't have a present

to give you," Melinda said, sadly.

Gingerbeard roared with laughter.

"Sproggobbler's teddy...

...is the best present I have

ever been given! But the

most wonderful of all is you two,"

he said, squeezing them both in his arms.

"Tomorrow I will take you both on

my ship and this time Melinda can

be the captain!"

"I am Melinda the Terrible, daughter of Gingerbeard, granddaughter of Blackbeard and great-granddaughter of Redbeard," Melinda chanted, following her dad.

"I am Ricky the Terror, brother of Melinda the Terrible and son of Gingerbeard!" Ricky shouted after her.

"Adventures ahoy!" Fatbeak added as he flew after them.

Franklin Watts
First published in Great Britain in 2015 by
The Watts Publishing Group

© RAGEOT-EDITEUR Paris, 2010
First published in French as
Fille De Pirate

Translation © Franklin Watts 2015
English text and adaptation by Fabrice
Blanchefort.

Series Editor: Melanie Palmer
Series Advisor: Catherine Glavina
Cover Designer: Cathryn Gilbert
Design Manager: Peter Scoulding

A CIP catalogue record for this book is
available from the British Library.

ISBN 978 1 4451 3710 0 (hbk)
ISBN 978 1 4451 3713 1 (pbk)
ISBN 978 1 4451 3711 7 (ebook)
ISBN 978 1 4451 3712 4 (library ebook)

Printed in China

Franklin Watts
An imprint of
Hachette Children's Group
Part of The Watts Publishing Group
Carmelite House
50 Victoria Embankment
London EC4Y 0DZ

An Hachette UK Company
www.hachette.co.uk

www.franklinwatts.co.uk